FLUFFY®
AND FRIENDS

by **Kate McMullan**

Illustrated by **Mavis Smith**

Scholastic Reader — Level 3

SCHOLASTIC INC. Cartwheel ·B·O·O·K·S·®

New York   Toronto   London   Auckland   Sydney
Mexico City   New Delhi   Hong Kong   Buenos Aires

For Tommy, Jessica, and Nicholas Donato
— K.M.

To Matthew and Ross
— M.S.

The author would like to offer many thanks to all the firefighters
of Ladder Company 7 and Engine Company 16 of the
New York City Fire Department, especially Tommy Donato and
Mike Boccia for their time and for their excellent suggestions,
which found their way into this story.

Fluffy and the Firefighters (0-439-12917-6)
Text copyright © 1999 by Kate McMullan.
Illustrations copyright © 1999 by Mavis Smith.

Fluffy Meets the Tooth Fairy (0-439-12918-4)
Text copyright © 2000 by Kate McMullan.
Illustrations copyright © 2000 by Mavis Smith.

Fluffy Grows a Garden (0-439-20674-X)
Text copyright © 2001 by Kate McMullan.
Illustrations copyright © 2001 by Mavis Smith.
Activities copyright © 2003 by Scholastic Inc.

Fluffy Goes Apple Picking (0-439-31420-8)
Text copyright © 2001 by Kate McMullan.
Illustrations copyright © 2001 by Mavis Smith.
Activities copyright © 2003 by Scholastic Inc.

Fluffy's Spring Vacation (0-590-37217-3)
Text copyright © 1998 by Kate McMullan.
Illustrations copyright © 1998 by Mavis Smith.
Activities copyright © 2003 by Scholastic Inc.

All rights reserved. Published by Scholastic Inc.
SCHOLASTIC, CARTWHEEL BOOKS, FLUFFY THE CLASSROOM GUINEA PIG,
and associated logos are trademarks and/or registered trademarks
of Scholastic Inc.

12 11 10 9 8 7 6 5 4 3 2   6 7 8 9/0

Printed in Singapore   10

This edition created exclusively for Barnes & Noble, Inc.

2004 Barnes & Noble Books

ISBN 0-7607-5821-2

First Compilation printing, July 2004

FLUFFY®
AND THE FIREFIGHTERS

by Kate McMullan • Illustrated by Mavis Smith

Save the Pig!

Firefighter Tom and Firefighter Mike
came to Ms. Day's classroom.

"Hello, firefighters!" said all the kids.
Fluffy did not say anything.
He was having his morning nap.

"Hi, kids," said Firefighter Tom.

"We are here to tell you about our job.

Our uniforms help to protect us

when we fight fires. We wear turnout coats

and high rubber boots," Tom told the class.

Mike put on his turnout coat.

He stepped into his high rubber boots.

Fluffy turned over in his sleep.

"We wear thick gloves, too," said Tom.

Mike pulled on his thick gloves.

"We wear helmets to protect our heads," said Tom.

Mike put on his helmet.

"His helmet has a flashlight on it," Emma whispered to Wade.

"That helps him see in the dark."

Fluffy did not see anything.

He was in dreamland.

"Breathing too much smoke
makes people sick," said Firefighter Tom.
"So firefighters breathe air from
tanks on their backs."
Firefighter Mike put on his air tank.

He put a big mask over his face.

A hose connected the mask to the tank.

"Now Mike can breathe air

from the air tank," said Tom.

"Now he is ready to fight a fire."

"Hooray for firefighters!" said Maxwell.

Everyone clapped and cheered.

The cheering woke Fluffy.
He opened his eyes.
He saw Firefighter Mike.
Help! thought Fluffy.
A space monster has landed!
Call the police! Call the Marines!
Somebody save the pig!

Fluffy ran around his cage.
He squeaked and squeaked.
"I think Fluffy is scared of Mike,"
said Jasmine.
"Firefighters can look scary
when they are dressed to fight fires,"
Tom told the class.
"But firefighters are your friends."

Help! Help! thought Fluffy.
Mars invader!
Somebody save the pig!
Fluffy dove under his food dish.
"Fluffy is hiding from Mike,"
said Maxwell.

"If a firefighter comes to help you,"
said Tom, "do not go under your bed
or into a closet. Never ever hide
from a firefighter."

Firefighter? thought Fluffy.

He peeked out from under his food bowl.

Did someone say *firefighter*?

Firefighter Mike took off his mask.

"Hello, Fluffy," he said.

"Don't be scared of me."

Me? Scared? thought Fluffy.

Ha! You must be joking!

Fluffy's Wild Ride

"Our fire engine is parked outside,"
Tom told Ms. Day's class.
"Come and see it."
Everyone went outside.
Wade brought Fluffy, too.

"Firefighter Carolina drives the fire engine,"
said Tom. "We call her the *chauffeur*."
"Hi, kids," said Carolina. She waved.
All the kids waved back.
Fluffy waved, too.

"A fire engine is also called a pumper,"
said Mike. "It pumps water
from a fire hydrant through hoses."
Very cool, thought Fluffy.
I bet I could drive this fire engine.
I bet I could be a firefighter.

Firefighters Tom and Mike let the kids
sit in the cab of the fire engine.
Wade was last in line.
"Hot dog!" said Wade
when his turn finally came.

He climbed into the cab.
He put Fluffy down on the seat.
Wade looked at all the dials.
He pretended to steer the engine.

Then Wade climbed out of the cab.

He ran to get in line to hold a fire hose.

He forgot about Fluffy.

Fluffy was alone in the cab
of the fire engine.

All right! thought Fluffy.

I am a firefighter now!

Firefighter Fluffy
drove the fire engine fast.
He made the siren wail: *Whoop! Whoop!*
He honked the horn: *Beeeeeep! Beeeeeep!*
All the cars got out of the way.
Fluffy pulled up to the curb.
A store was on fire!

Fluffy connected a hose to a fire hydrant.

He aimed the hose at the fire.

Water shot from the nozzle: *Whoooosh!*

In no time, he put the fire out.

Fluffy! cried the guinea pigs.

You are our hero!

Nothing to it, said Fluffy.

Suddenly, Fluffy felt the fire
engine lurch. Firefighter Carolina
had jumped into the driver's seat.
She drove away from the school.
She zoomed around a corner.
Wow! thought Fluffy. **This is fast!**
Fluffy felt his breakfast gurgling
in his tummy.
He was not sure he liked going so fast.

Firefighter Carolina put on the siren.

WHOOP! WHOOP! WHOOP!

Yikes! thought Fluffy.

Carolina honked the horn.

BEEEEEEP! BEEEEEEP!

Jeepers! thought Fluffy.

He was not sure he liked so much noise.

The engine pulled up to a fire.
Fluffy felt the heat from the flames.
He was not sure he liked being so hot.
Fluffy was not sure he wanted to be
a firefighter after all.

A ladder truck pulled up next to the engine.
The firefighters began fighting the fire.
They worked as a team.
Some firefighters climbed tall ladders.
Some cut a hole in the roof
to let out the smoke.

Some ran into the building
to search for people
who might be trapped inside.
Some held hoses from up high in a bucket.
They fought the fire for a long time.

Fluffy watched from the fire engine.

He saw that the firefighters were very brave.

He saw how the firefighters
worked together as a team.

Now he wished he could be part
of a firefighting team.

Firefighters are real heroes,
thought Fluffy.

But how can a pig fight fires?

Firefighter Fluffy

At last Firefighters Tom, Mike, and Carolina
came back to the fire engine.
They put away their equipment.
Then they got into the cab.

Their faces were hot
and smudged with smoke.
Fluffy thought they looked tired.
But he thought they looked happy, too.
After all, they had put out a fire.
And they had saved people's lives.

"Well, look who's here," said Firefighter Tom.
He picked up Fluffy.

"Hi, Fluffy," said Mike.

"Fluffy," said Carolina, "are you trying to tell
us that you want to be a firefighter?"

You got that right, said Fluffy.

But how can I be a firefighter?

Carolina drove back to the firehouse.

Tom carried Fluffy inside.

He called Ms. Day.

He told her where he had found
Firefighter Fluffy.

"Firefighter Fluffy!" Ms. Day laughed.

"I will tell my students about that.

May I bring them to the firehouse
this afternoon to pick up Fluffy?"

"Fine," said Tom. "See you then!"

Firefighter Tom carried Fluffy down the hall.

"Spike!" called Tom. "You have company!"

Uh-oh, thought Fluffy. **Who is Spike?**

"Spike" did not sound like a firefighter.

But then, neither did "Fluffy."

Then Fluffy saw Spike.

He was a big white dog with black spots.

He was curled up on his bed.

Spike opened one eye.

Good Spike, thought Fluffy. **Nice doggie**.

Firefighter Tom held Fluffy next to Spike.

Spike sniffed Fluffy.

Fluffy sniffed Spike.

Then Tom put Fluffy down beside Spike.

Spike did not seem to mind.

Neither did Fluffy.

After all, it had been quite a morning.

Fluffy was ready for his afternoon nap.

Maybe he could not be a firefighter.

But he could always dream.

"Wake up, Firefighter Fluffy!"
a voice said.
Fluffy's eyes popped open.
He saw Ms. Day and the whole class.
"We made firefighter posters," said Wade.

Everyone held a poster.

Every poster had a picture of Fluffy on it.

"Good work!" Tom told Ms. Day's class.

"Now Fluffy is a firefighter after all!"

Yes! thought Firefighter Fluffy.
**The best way to fight fires
is to keep them from happening
in the first place!**

MEETS
THE TOOTH FAIRY

For Charlotte,
who will have many visits from the tooth fairy
—K.M.

For the kids at Camp Heartland
—M.S.

FLUFFY®
MEETS
THE TOOTH FAIRY

by Kate McMullan • Illustrated by Mavis Smith

Fluffy's Loose Tooth

"I have a loose tooth, Fluffy,"
said Wade. He wiggled his tooth.
Yikes! thought Fluffy.

"It will fall out," said Wade.
"And I will put it under my pillow.
When I am asleep, the tooth fairy will
come and take my tooth. And she will
leave me a present."
She will? thought Fluffy.

Fluffy liked presents.

He wondered if he had a loose tooth.

He tried to wiggle his right front tooth.

It was not loose.

He tried to wiggle his left front tooth.

It was not loose—or was it?

Maybe it *was* a little bit loose.

Jared came over to Fluffy's cage with
Mr. Lee's class pet, Kiss.
Wade wiggled his tooth for Jared.
"Cool," said Jared. He put Kiss down
in Fluffy's cage.
"My cousin lost her tooth," Jared said.
"The tooth fairy left her a comic book."

I have a loose tooth, Fluffy told Kiss.

You do not, said Kiss.

Yes, I do, said Fluffy.

It will fall out and I will put it under my pillow. The tooth fairy will take my tooth and leave me a present.

Kiss rolled her eyes.

You do not have a pillow, she said.

Wade was doing tricks with his
loose tooth. He closed his mouth
and made his loose tooth stick
out between his lips.
"Gross!" said Jared.

And, Kiss said, **guinea pig teeth
do not fall out. We gnaw on things
to wear down our teeth.**

With his tongue, Wade pulled his tooth
all the way back.
"Yuck," said Jared.
"I can see the insides of your tooth!"

If we did not gnaw, our teeth would grow so long we could not eat, said Kiss.
Yuck! thought Fluffy.

"Wade!" Jared cried suddenly.
"Your tooth is gone!"

The boys looked on the table
and on the floor.
"You must have swallowed it,"
said Jared.
"Do you think the tooth fairy will
bring me a present?" Wade asked.
Jared shook his head.
"No tooth, no present."

The Lost L

It was Wade's
Fluffy home
Jared helped v.
cage out to the car.
Wade's sister Zoe sat in th.
Wade and Fluffy sat in the back.

ost my tooth!" Wade said.
wallowed it. Will the tooth
still leave me a present?"
ite the tooth fairy a note,"
id Mom, "and put it under your
pillow. The tooth fairy understands
about lost lost teeth."

Zoe turned around in her seat.

"No tooth, no present," she whispered.

Tooth or no tooth, Fluffy hoped the tooth
fairy would leave Wade a present.

That night, Wade wrote a note. He read it to Fluffy:

Dear Tooth Fairy,
My tooth came out today, but I must have swallowed it. So I cannot leave it under my pillow. Can you please leave me a present anyway?

Your friend, Wade

Wade got into his bed and put the note
under his pillow.
"Good night, Fluffy," said Wade.

Fluffy turned around in his hay.
He thought about Wade's tooth.
He hoped Jared and Zoe were wrong about
"no tooth, no present."

Fluffy made himself a fine hole
in the hay and lay down.
Ouch! Something stuck him.
Fluffy jumped up. He dug in the hay.

At last he saw what had stuck him.

Well, well, well, thought Fluffy.
I found the lost lost tooth.

Fluffy Meets the Tooth Fairy

Fluffy squealed and whistled. But he could not wake Wade up.

It's up to me to get this tooth under his pillow, thought Fluffy.

Fluffy turned his food bowl upside down.
He put his cardboard box on top of it.
He put his tunnel on top of that.

Fluffy picked up Wade's tooth and
climbed up, up, up.
At the tip top, Fluffy rocked and wobbled.
Stay cool, pig, thought Fluffy.

Fluffy squeezed his eyes shut.
And down he went.

BOP! He landed on Wade's desk.

He put the tooth in his mouth
and climbed down.

At last Fluffy's feet touched the floor.
All right! he thought. **This pig is
on his way!**
Fluffy was running toward Wade's bed
when he heard a noise.
Is it the tooth fairy? he wondered.

No, it was a cat!
Fluffy hit the ground. He grabbed the
corner of Wade's rug and rolled.
When he stopped, the cat looked in at
Fluffy and Fluffy looked out at the cat.
They looked at each other for a long time.

At last Zoe called, "Brutus! Snack time!"

Brutus zoomed off.

Fluffy rolled the other way.

He rolled himself out of the rug,

and ran to Wade's bed as fast as he could.

Fluffy grabbed a corner of Wade's sheet
and climbed up. And very carefully,
he slipped the tooth under Wade's pillow.
Yes! thought Fluffy. **The pig did it!**

Fluffy was tired. He needed some rest
before he started back to his cage.
He burrowed under the blanket, put his
head on the pillow, and closed his eyes.

The next thing he knew,
the tooth fairy showed up.
**Wow! She looks just like Kiss in
a tutu!** thought Fluffy.
Move it, buddy, she growled. **I can't
lift this pillow with you on it.**

Fluffy jumped up. The tooth fairy lifted
the pillow and grabbed Wade's tooth.
Got it! she cried.
She added it to her necklace made of teeth.

I'm out of here, the tooth fairy said.

Hold it! said Fluffy. **What about**

Wade's present?

The tooth fairy rolled her eyes.

Oh, all right, she said.

She pushed two coins under the pillow.

**I put the tooth there. How about a
present for me?** said Fluffy.
It wasn't *your* tooth, she said.
No tooth, no present!

Fluffy rolled off the pillow and woke up.
Was that a bad dream? he wondered.
Just then Fluffy saw something
twinkling above Wade's pillow.
It looked like blue and yellow sparks.
This is a good dream, thought Fluffy.
And he closed his eyes again.

"Fluffy!" Wade called.

Fluffy's eyes popped open.

He was back in his cage.

How had he gotten there?

He had no idea.

"The tooth fairy came!" said Wade.

No kidding, Fluffy thought.

"She left me two quarters!" said Wade.

"And look. She left a present for you."

For me? thought Fluffy.
Wade put a piece of green pepper
into Fluffy's cage.
Fluffy bit into the pepper.
It was sweet and crunchy.

Mmmm, thought Fluffy as he chewed.
No tooth, yes present!

FLUFFY®
GROWS A GARDEN

FLUFFY®
GROWS A GARDEN

by Kate McMullan · Illustrated by Mavis Smith

I Love Carrots!

"Spring is here," said Ms. Day.

"What happens in the spring?"

"Spring vacation!" said Emma.

"Baseball spring training!" said Wade.

"Plants start to grow," said Maxwell.

"Yes," said Ms. Day.

"This spring we will plant a garden."

Plant carrots! thought Fluffy.

I love carrots!

Everyone in the class
filled paper cups with soil.
They planted seeds in the cups.
They watered the seeds.

"Ms. Day?" said Emma and Jasmine.

"May we plant a garden for Fluffy?"

"Good idea," said Ms. Day.

Great idea! thought Fluffy.

Plant a carrot garden!

The girls took three cups
over to Fluffy's cage.
"What kinds of seeds shall we plant?"
said Emma.
Take a wild guess, thought Fluffy.

"How about marigolds?" said Emma.

Wrong! thought Fluffy.

I can't eat flowers!

Emma and Jasmine planted
marigold seeds.

"Do you like peas, Fluffy?" asked Emma.

Not as much as carrots,
thought Fluffy.

The girls planted pea seeds.

"Now what?" said Jasmine.

Read my lips, thought Fluffy.

CARROT SEEDS!

"Petunias?" said Emma.

No! No! No! thought Fluffy.

He raced over to his food bowl.

He picked up what was left

of a carrot top.

He ran with it over to the girls.

"Yuck," said Jasmine.

"Fluffy brought us his old carrot."

"Hey, I know," said Emma.

"Let's plant carrot seeds for Fluffy."

Bingo! thought Fluffy.

The girls planted carrot seeds.

Emma watered the seeds.
She put the seed cups
into Fluffy's cage.
Grow, carrots! thought Fluffy.

For a while, nothing grew.
Then, one day, green shoots
peeked out of the soil.
They grew bigger and bigger.
Leaves appeared.

These plants are green,
thought Fluffy.
Carrots are orange.
Who stole my carrots?

One sunny day,
Emma carried Fluffy's plants outside.
Jasmine carried Fluffy.
She put him down in the class garden.

Emma dug three holes.
She slid Fluffy's plants out of the cups
and planted them in the holes.
Jasmine watered Fluffy's plants.
Don't water me! thought Fluffy.
I'm not a plant!

Emma wrote the names of the plants
on craft sticks.
She poked the sticks into the soil.
"This is your marigold," she told Fluffy.
"And this is your pea plant."
Big deal, thought Fluffy.

"This is your carrot plant," said Emma.

That? thought Fluffy. **I don't think so.**

"You know carrots grow underground, right, Fluffy?" said Jasmine.

Underground? thought Fluffy.
Uh...I knew that...
because I love carrots!

The Guard of the Garden

On sunny days,
the girls put Fluffy in the garden.
He liked to watch his plants
grow and change.
The marigold grew buds and flowers.
So did the pea plant.
The carrot plant got very bushy.

One day two bees
flew into the garden.
I am the guard of the garden!
Fluffy told the bees. **Buzz off!**
Hold it, pal, said the big bee.
Your garden needs us.

I land on a flower, see?
said the big bee.
While I drink nectar,
my legs get covered in pollen.
Then I visit another flower.
The pollen from the first flower
brushes off my legs
and onto the second flower.
Now the second flower can make
new seeds.

No bees, no seeds,
said the little bee.
Okay, bees, said Fluffy.
Come into my garden.

Fluffy saw two ladybugs.

I am the guard of the garden!

Fly away home! he told the ladybugs.

Not so fast, pig, said the big ladybug.

Your garden needs us.

See those little white bugs on

your pea plant?

Fluffy ran over to his pea plant.
He gasped!
The leaves were covered
with little white bugs.

Those bugs will suck the food out of the leaves, said the big ladybug.
Unless we eat the bugs first, said the little ladybug.
Hurry, ladybugs! said Fluffy.
Save my pea plant!

Fluffy saw a pair of worms.
I am the guard of the garden!
Fluffy told the worms. **Be gone!**

Peace, dude, said the big worm.
Your garden needs us.

We crawl around under the ground,
said the big worm.
We mix air into the soil.
The air makes space for water
to trickle down into the ground.

Down like where carrots grow, dude,
said the little worm.
Carrots? said Fluffy.
Welcome to my garden, worms!

Fluffy lay down
in the shade of his pea plant.
Fluffy watched the bees fly.
He watched the ladybugs eat.
He watched the worms crawl.
Gardening is hard work,
thought Fluffy.
But somebody's got to do it.

PEPPERS

Nice Work, Fluffy!

The days grew warm.
The marigold plant
was covered with flowers.
The pea flowers
had turned into pea pods.
The leaves of the carrot plant were
bigger than ever.
My garden is just right,
thought Fluffy.

Then Fluffy saw two slugs.

They were chewing on his pea plant.

He ran over to them.

I am the guard of the garden!

Fluffy told the slugs.

How does my garden need you?

Burp, said the big slug.

BURP, said the little slug.

The slugs kept chewing.

Scram, slugs! said Fluffy.

And I mean NOW!

He ran at the slugs.

The slimy slugs crawled away.

Emma picked Fluffy up.

"Nice work, Fluffy," she said.

Just doing my job, thought Fluffy.

"Now it is time to harvest the garden,"
Emma said.

Do what? thought Fluffy.

Emma began picking marigolds.

Stop! thought Fluffy.

Jasmine began picking pea pods.

Help! thought Fluffy.

Somebody call the police!

Then Emma reached down.

She took hold of the carrot plant.

What do you think you're doing?

thought Fluffy.

He ran at Emma.

But he was too late.

POP!

Emma pulled up a great big carrot.

Wow! thought Fluffy. **My carrot!**

Ms. Day's class had a feast.
They had a salad with lettuce and
tomatoes.
They had stuffed peppers.
They had mint iced tea.
Almost everything they ate
came from their garden.

Emma and Jasmine
set a place for Fluffy, too.
He had a little pot of marigolds.
He had seven peas.
And he had his great big carrot.
"Dig in, Fluffy," said Emma.

Yum! thought Fluffy.

He could hardly wait to grow
another carrot next spring.

FLUFFY®
GOES
APPLE PICKING

For my #1 Fluffy Consultant, Abraham Axler,
and his classmates,
and his teacher, Ms. Davis, at P.S. 87.
— K.M.

To Dad, who knew a good apple when he saw one.
— M.S.

FLUFFY
GOES
APPLE PICKING

by Kate McMullan • Illustrated by Mavis Smith

I Love Apples!

School was almost over for the day.
Fluffy was napping.
"We will have a picnic tomorrow,"
Ms. Day told her class,
"when we go . . ."

"Apple picking!" everyone called.

That woke Fluffy up.

Apples? he thought. **I love apples!**

"We will go to an orchard,"
said Ms. Day. "We will see
hundreds of apple trees and
thousands of apples."
Thousands? thought Fluffy.
His eyes grew wide.
**Who knew there were THAT
many apples?**

"We will pick apples from the apple trees," said Ms. Day. "Then what will we do with some of the apples?"

"Eat them!" everyone called.

Oh, yum! thought Fluffy.

I love apples!

"Ms. Day?" said Wade.

"Can Fluffy come apple picking, too?"

Can he? thought Fluffy. **I mean,
can I? Can I? PLEASE?**

"Of course, he can," said Ms. Day.

"Fluffy loves apples."

Right! thought Fluffy.

I L - O - V - E apples!

Just then, Lina from Mr. Lee's class
came through the door.
She was holding Kiss.

"Kiss's cage is a mess," said Lina.

I'll bet, thought Fluffy.

"Mr. Lee wants to give it
a good cleaning," said Lina.

"Can Kiss have a sleepover
with Fluffy tonight?"

No way! thought Fluffy.

"Sure," said Ms. Day.

Lina put Kiss into Fluffy's cage.

Kiss ran over to Fluffy's food bowl.
She started eating Fluffy's food.
Good-bye supper, thought Fluffy.
But he was too excited
about apple picking to be mad.

Kiss ate every bit of Fluffy's food.

Then she ran over to a pile of paper.

Hey! That's *my* bed, said Fluffy.

Too bad, said Kiss.

Fluffy crawled into his tube.

He was not happy

that Kiss had taken his bed.

But he was too excited

about apple picking to be mad.

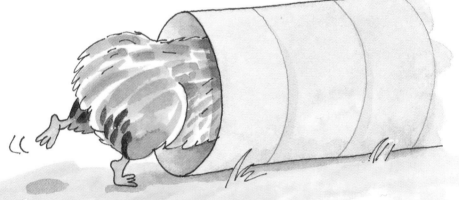

Fluffy closed his eyes.

But he could not fall asleep.

For one thing, he was hungry.

And Kiss was snoring:

honk-brrrrr, honk-brrrrr.

But that's not what kept Fluffy

awake. He was too excited

about apple picking to sleep.

Fluffy tried counting apples.
One apple, two apples,
three apples, he counted.
But even that did not help.
At last the sun came up.
Fluffy had been awake all night long.
Apples! thought Fluffy.
They can wear a pig out.

Kiss Goes Apple Picking

Ms. Day and the kids came
into the classroom.
Emma and Wade
ran over to Fluffy's cage.
"Fluffy doesn't look so good," said Emma.
"He looks sleepy," said Wade.

"Kiss looks wide awake," said Wade.

"Let's take her apple picking, too."

What? thought Fluffy.

"A friend for Fluffy," said Emma.

"What a good idea!"

Not really, thought Fluffy.

"Come on, sleepy Fluffy,"
said Emma.
She picked him up and
carried him to the bus.
Wade carried Kiss.

The bus drove to the orchard.
Everyone got out
and ran to the apple trees.
"Fluffy is too sleepy to pick apples,"
said Emma.
Wrong! thought Fluffy.

"You can still have fun, Fluffy,"
said Emma. "You can watch Kiss
pick apples."
You must be joking! thought Fluffy.

Kiss picked another apple.
She ate it up. Then she ate
another one. And another!
"Too bad you are too sleepy
to eat an apple, Fluffy," said Emma.
I could never be THAT sleepy,
thought Fluffy.

Wade put Kiss into a basket
of apples.
"Have all you want!" he said.
Kiss started chomping the apples.
Fluffy could not believe his eyes.
Kiss was an apple-eating machine!

Fluffy jumped out of Emma's hands.

He ran for the basket of apples.

Look out, Kiss! he thought.

Here I come!

He took a flying leap!

He banged into his food bowl.

Ow! thought Fluffy.

"Fluffy!" said Emma.

"Are you all right?"

Fluffy looked around.

He was in his cage.

He did not see any apples.

"You were dreaming," said Emma.

Fluffy heard a terrible groan.

He turned and saw Kiss.

She was lying on her back,

holding her tummy.

Ooooh, said Kiss.

Your food made me sick!

"Kiss doesn't look so good,"
said Emma.
"Maybe she ate too much," said Wade.
"I'll take her back to Mr. Lee."
Emma picked up Fluffy.
"Let's go apple picking," she said.
All right! thought Fluffy.
Let's go!

Fluffy Goes Apple Picking

Ms. Day's class rode to the orchard.

Everyone got off the bus.

Fluffy sniffed the air.

Smells like apples! he thought.

When do we eat?

"Welcome to Hill Orchard!"
a man said. "I'm Mr. Hill.
And who is this?"
he asked when he saw Fluffy.
"This is Fluffy," said Emma.
"He's one fine pig," said Mr. Hill.
That's me! thought Fluffy.

Mr. Hill picked Fluffy up
and put him on his shoulder.
"One fine pig needs
one fine apple," he said.
When? thought Fluffy.
How about now?

"Climb into the wagon," Mr. Hill
told the kids. "I will pull you
to the top of the hill with my tractor.
Apples grow best on hilltops."
Everyone climbed into the wagon.
Go, Mr. Hill! thought Fluffy.
Get me to those apples!

Mr. Hill drove past a big red barn.
"I grow Macintosh apples," he said.
"I grow Fuji apples, too. I also grow
a kind called Granny Smith."
I'll have one of each! thought Fluffy.

Mr. Hill stopped at the top of the hill.

Everyone jumped out of the wagon.

Mr. Hill passed out baskets.

"Fill these up with apples!" he said.

Hey, Mr. Hill! thought Fluffy.

**How about filling ME up
with apples?**

Mr. Hill walked around the orchard.
Fluffy rode on his shoulder.
"Eat while you pick," said Mr. Hill.
"There is nothing as good as
an apple right off the tree."
Emma bit into an apple: *CHOMP!*
What does a pig have to do
around here to get an apple?
thought Fluffy.

"Okay, pig," said Mr. Hill. "Your turn."

He held Fluffy up to a branch.

Fluffy grabbed an apple. He pulled.

Nothing happened.

He pulled harder.

Nothing happened.

Fluffy pulled with all his might.

All of a sudden,

Fluffy slipped out of Mr. Hill's hand.

"Oops!" said Mr. Hill.

The branch snapped back fast,

and the apple went flying.

So did Fluffy.

AAAAAHHHHHHH!!!! thought Fluffy.

Fluffy landed with a *THUMP!*
Ms. Day turned and saw Fluffy
sitting in her apple basket.
"Fluffy!" she said.
"Where did *you* come from?"

I'll tell you later, thought Fluffy.
Right now, I've got an apple to eat.
He took a bite: *CHOMP!*

Mr. Hill drove everyone down the hill.
Ms. Day spread a cloth on the ground.
She passed around bread and cheese.
Mr. Hill poured apple cider.
All the kids ate the apples
that they had picked themselves.
Fluffy did, too. **Mm-mm!** he thought.
This is one fine picnic.

After the picnic,
everyone lined up for a picture.
"Say 'apples'!" said Mr. Hill.
"Wait!" said Emma. "I have a better
idea. Let's say, 'Fluffy'!"
Everyone yelled, "FLUFFY!"

It was one fine picture.

SPRING VACATION

To Marie-France Roche
— K.M.

To Gabriel
— M.S.

FLUFFY'S
SPRING VACATION

by Kate McMullan • Illustrated by Mavis Smith

Fluffy the Brave

"Who will take Fluffy home
for spring vacation?" asked Ms. Day.
"I will," said Emma.
"But you have a cat, Emma," said Ms. Day.
"Fluffy would be afraid of a cat."
Wrong! thought Fluffy.
I'm not afraid of anything!

"I have two cats," said Emma.
"And a dog. But they are old.
All they do is sleep.
They won't hurt Fluffy."

So Fluffy went home with Emma.

"The brown cat is Jack," Emma told Fluffy.

"The orange one is Jill."

Nice kitties, thought Fluffy.

"This is Skippy," Emma said.

Woof! Woof! thought Fluffy.

That night, Emma and Fluffy
had a tea party.
Then Fluffy went to sleep under his straw.

In the middle of the night,

Fluffy heard a noise.

He opened his eyes.

Four big yellow eyes were looking at him.

Yikes! thought Fluffy.

I'm having a bad dream!

But it wasn't a dream.

It was Jack and Jill.

Don't mess with me, cats, said Fluffy.

Jack patted the door of Fluffy's cage
with his paw.
The door opened.
You are asking for trouble, said Fluffy.

Jill poked her paw into the cage
and pulled Fluffy out the door.
You'll be sorry! said Fluffy.

Jill picked Fluffy up and
carried him into the living room.
She put him down on the floor.
I have sharp teeth, Fluffy told Jack.
Jack showed Fluffy his sharp teeth.
I have sharp claws, Fluffy told Jill.
Jill stuck out her sharp claws.

Okay, cats, said Fluffy. **Look out!**

Fluffy ran at Jill.

He jumped at Jack.

He ran and jumped and growled.

Fluffy did not see Skippy come up behind him.

But Jack and Jill did.

Their eyes got very big and they ran away.

I told you not to mess with me, cats!

Fluffy called after them.

Then Fluffy turned around.

He saw Skippy.

Don't be afraid, Skippy, said Fluffy.

I scared the cats away.

Fluffy did not know
how to get back to his cage.
So he followed Skippy to his bed.
Fluffy lay down beside the dog.
Wake me up if the cats come back,
Fluffy told Skippy.
I will take care of them.
Then Fluffy the Brave fell asleep.

Fluffy the Explorer

"I'm going to get a haircut,"
Emma told Fluffy.
"Dad says you can come, too."
Why? said Fluffy. **My hair is
just right.**
Emma put Fluffy in a shoe box
and off they went.

They walked into Sandy's Haircuts.

"Will you watch Fluffy?" Emma asked.

"Sure," said her dad.

Emma went to get her hair washed.

Her dad sat down.

He put the shoe box on a chair.

Then he started reading.

Fluffy sat up.

He looked in the mirror.

He saw so many guinea pigs!

Fluffy climbed out of his box.

Follow me, pigs! said Fluffy the Explorer.

We will go where no pigs have gone before!

Fluffy saw a mountain.

He started climbing.

He went up and up.

But the mountain started shaking.

Earthquake! cried Fluffy the Explorer.

Hold on, pigs!

The earthquake tossed Fluffy
into the dark.
We must get out of this cave!
said Fluffy the Explorer.
Follow me, pigs!
Fluffy jumped out of the cave.

Just in time, too.

The ice is slick, said Fluffy the Explorer.

Watch out, pigs!

Fluffy led the way over the ice.

What's this? thought Fluffy the Explorer.
It was a big silver thing.
Inside was a monster!
The monster started to roar!
Jump, pigs! cried Fluffy the Explorer.
Fluffy jumped down.

But the monster was after him!
Run, pigs! cried Fluffy the Explorer.
Run for your lives!
Fluffy ran under a big rock.

Emma showed her dad her short hair.

Then she picked up the shoe box.

"Dad!" she cried. "Fluffy's gone!"

"What?" said her dad.

Emma dropped the shoe box.

"Fluffy!" she called. "Where are you?"

"Here, Fluffy," called Emma's dad.

Fluffy saw that the monster was far away.

He saw the shoe box on the floor.

Follow me, pigs! said Fluffy the Explorer.

He ran out from under the rock

and jumped in the box.

We did it! said Fluffy the Explorer.

Good work, pigs!

Emma came back and sat down.
She looked in the box.
"Fluffy!" she cried. "Where have
you been?"
It's a long story, thought Fluffy the
Explorer.

Fluffy Shows Up

"Good night, Fluffy," said Emma.
"Tomorrow we go back to school."
Fluffy went to sleep.
But in the middle of the night,
a noise woke him up.
Jack and Jill were back.
Not again! thought Fluffy.

Jack opened Fluffy's cage.
Jill got Fluffy out.
But this time Fluffy took off!

Fluffy ran out of Emma's room.
Jack and Jill ran after him.

Fluffy raced down the hallway.
Jack and Jill raced after him.

Fluffy zoomed around a corner.
He heard the cats behind him.
Fluffy saw a bag by the front door.
It was open at the top.
Fluffy ran and jumped into the bag.

He peeked out.

He saw the cats run by.

Heh heh, thought Fluffy.

Then Fluffy found a soft place
inside the bag and fell asleep.

The next morning, Emma cried,
"Fluffy's gone!"
"Not again!" said Emma's dad.
"I have a big meeting this morning,"
said Emma's mom. "I have to catch a plane."
"Go on," said Emma's dad. "Emma and I
will find Fluffy."
Emma's mom kissed Emma good-bye.
"Don't worry," she said. "Fluffy will show up.
He always does." Then she picked up
her briefcase and ran out the door.

Emma's dad drove Emma to school.
"What will I say about Fluffy?"
Emma asked him.
"Say that Fluffy will show up,"
said her dad. "He always does."

At the airport, Emma's mom waited in line. Then she put her purse and her briefcase on the X-ray machine.

She walked through the gate.

"Stop," a guard told her.

"You can't bring an animal on the plane."

"An animal?" said Emma's mom.

"What do you mean?"

The guard showed Emma's mom the X ray.

The X ray showed Fluffy.

Emma's mom took Fluffy out of her briefcase.

"What are YOU doing here?" she asked.

Beats me, thought Fluffy.

So, what's for breakfast?

"I'll be back," Emma's mom told the guard.

She ran outside.

She waved down a taxi.

"Driver?" she said. "This is Fluffy."

And she told him what happened.

"Leave Fluffy to me," the driver said.

At school, Emma said, "Ms. Day?
I have something to tell the class."
"Okay," said Ms. Day.
Emma walked to the front of the room.
"Uh...," she said. "This is about Fluffy."

Fluffy liked riding in the taxi.
Faster, driver! he thought.

"But Fluffy was not in his cage,"
Emma was saying.
"Look!" called Wade. "A taxi!"
All the kids looked out the window
as a taxi pulled up in front of the school.
The taxi driver came into Ms. Day's room.
"Here's Fluffy," he said.
"I hope he is not late for school."

"Fluffy!" said Emma. "You DID show up!"
I always do, thought Fluffy.